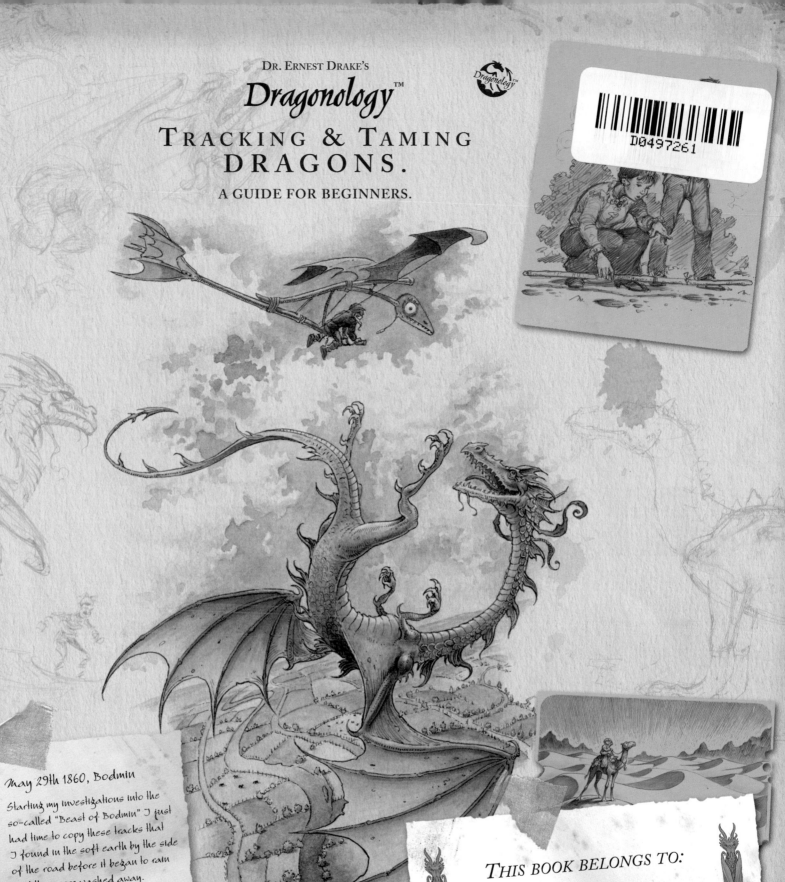

Dr. Ernest Drake's

Dragonology™

TRACKING & TAMING
DRAGONS.

A GUIDE FOR BEGINNERS.

May 29th 1860, Bodmin

Starting my investigations into the
so-called "Beast of Bodmin" I just
had time to copy these tracks that
I found in the soft earth by the side
of the road before it began to rain
and they were washed away.
I have a feeling that they were made
by Torcher in order to trick me. If
you look carefully, it is obvious that
they are the same footprint over and
over again. I wonder if he made
them by hopping?

THIS BOOK BELONGS TO:

~~Thomas~~

~~Degabriele.~~

EDITED BY

DUGALD A. STEER, B.A. (BRIST), S.A.S.D.

ILLUSTRATED.

THE TEMPLAR COMPANY:
PUBLISHERS OF RARE & UNUSUAL BOOKS.

CONTENTS.

First published in the UK in 2006 by Templar Publishing,
an imprint of The Templar Company plc,
Pippbrook Mill, London Road, Dorking, Surrey RH4 1JE, UK.

Illustrations copyright © 2006 by Douglas Carrel.
Text and design copyright © 2006 by The Templar Company plc.
Designed by Jonathan Lambert & Nghiem Ta.
Dragonology™ is a trademark of The Templar Company plc.
All Rights Reserved.
ISBN-13: 978-1-84011-579-6
ISBN-10: 1-84011-579-3
3 5 7 9 10 8 6 4 2
Manufactured in China.

PUBLISHER'S NOTE: This book purports to be the facsimile of an
original that was among the effects of Dr. Ernest Drake. It is possible
that he wrote it for two junior dragonologists who needed a little more
information than was to be found in *Dragonology—the Complete Book of
Dragons*, said to have been originally published in 1895, and
republished by Templar Publishing in 2003.

templar publishing

www.dragonology.com

An Introduction to Dragon Craft.

"Where can *I* find dragons?" is such a common refrain these days that it seems to crop up almost every time our favourite flying beasts are mentioned. It often gives rise to the counter-question, "But what would you do with them if you found them?" Bearing both of these questions in mind, the intrepid experts at the *Secret and Ancient Society of Dragonologists* [S.A.S.D.] decided to commission a brief guide which would cover the essentials of practical dragon craft in order to answer them as thoroughly and succinctly as possible, and *Tracking and Taming Dragons* is the result. The book starts with the wise advice that the best way to begin tracking dragons is to keep a lookout for the more obvious signs of recent dragon activity. It contains a veritable treasure hoard of useful information that will allow students to quickly progress with their tracking skills, and also to gain a useful working knowledge of the best methods of taming these wonderful creatures.

Ernest Drake

STARTING OUT.

Newcomers to dragon tracking are often surprised to find that they do not need to purchase an array of expensive equipment in order to pursue this interesting pastime. A stout pair of boots or shoes, appropriate clothes for the season and location are all that are required, along with a keen pair of eyes, a curious disposition and an unquenchable thirst for knowledge.

WHERE TO START TRACKING.
Until you become an expert, it is best to search for dragon tracks where they are likely to stand out.

In jungle and woodland, tracks may be most easily seen in the soft mud or sand by stream or river banks.

In snowy areas, dragon tracks are likely to be fresh, as they will be quickly covered by each new snowfall.

* *Sand dunes can be a particularly good place to begin searching in desert regions, unless it is windy.*

COMPARING DRAGON TRACKS.
Each species of dragon leaves their own tell-tale footprints which can help the student to quickly identify which sort of species has been discovered.

This is useful in making a risk-assessment of how safe it may be to approach any particular specimen.

KNUCKER TRACKS.
A. Fairly light marks left by dragon's foreclaws.
B. Long, thin toe marks.
C. Small, deep pad mark.
D. Prominent hind claw.

EUROPEAN TRACKS.
A. Deep, round holes left by long foreclaws.
B. Wide toe marks.
C. Wide, shallow pad mark.
D. Prominent hind claw.

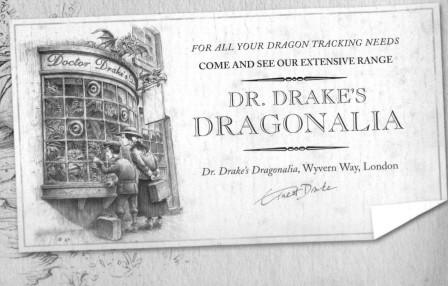

DRAGON HABITATS.

Having a working knowledge of different types of dragon habitat will enable the tracker to predict which kinds of dragons he is most likely to encounter. The tracker can then assess possible lair sites and other places that are likely to be frequented by dragons, such as streams or mountain peaks, and begin to search them for tracks and other signs such as scat [dragon droppings].

MOUNTAIN.

IN the West, hunt for caves among the higher tops; in the East, pay attention to areas around streams, lakes and waterfalls.

TYPES OF DRAGON—European [*draco occidentalis magnus*]; Chinese *Lung* [*draco orientalis magnus*]. TRACKS—May lead to lair or cave of European dragon, or favourite water source of *Lung*. SCAT—Large, smelly scat containing bones of prey [European]. No one has recorded *Lung* scat.

Japanese Lung *footprint.*

Lung dragon.

European dragon.

European dragon scat.

DESERT & SAVANNA.

A camel may be quite useful in following tracks in the desert. While tracking in the savanna, be careful to avoid being ambushed by lions.

TYPES OF DRAGON—Wyvern [*draco africanus*]; Lindworm [*draco serpentalis*]. TRACKS—Wyverns often leave their footprints in sandy areas; Lindworm tracks are usually obliterated by their own tails. SCAT—Large, containing remnants of prey [Wyvern]; long and thin [Lindworm].

Wyvern.

Wyvern scat.

Wyvern footprint.

ICY REGIONS.

IN Arctic and Antarctic regions beset by frequent blizzards, the tracker may only have a few hours before tracks disappear forever.

TYPE OF DRAGON—Frost [*draco occidentalis maritimus*]. TRACKS—Frost dragon tracks remain visible until new snow falls. SCAT—Fresh frost dragon scat is quite warm and, in Antarctic regions, quickly becomes adopted by groups of Emperor penguins seeking warmth.

Frost dragon footprint.

Frost dragon.

Frost dragon scat.

OUTBACK.

RATHER than track dragons in the outback, one effective method is to lure them to you by baiting natural features of the landscape.

TYPE OF DRAGON—Marsupial [*draco marsupialis*]. TRACKS—Due to the infrequency of rain in the Australian interior, marsupial tracks can be hard to age as they last so long. SCAT—The temperature of a dragon's scat is the best way to tell how recently the owner was last present.

Marsupial scat.

Marsupial footprints.

Marsupial.

JUNGLE.

PERHAPS the most difficult place to track dragons, due to its dense undergrowth and the likelihood of stubbing one's toe on Mex scat.

TYPE OF DRAGON—Amphithere [*draco americanus mex*]. TRACKS—The Mexican Amphithere [often known as the *amphiptere*] leaves snake-like tracks with its legless torso. SCAT—Soft and squishy when fresh, amphithere scat soon hardens to a stone-like consistency.

Mex scat.

Amphithere.

Mex tracks.

WOODLAND.

HUNT for knuckers in the early morning. They are often found breakfasting near rabbit warrens, or waiting by the side of lonely paths.

An ability to blend in with the natural environment so that the tracker becomes almost invisible may be a life-saver.

TYPE OF DRAGON—Knucker [*draco troglodytes*]. TRACKS—Knucker tracks are best sought in the mud or sand by the banks of streams or ponds. They are particularly hard to see in leaf mould. SCAT—Knucker scat has the appearance of large but irregularly sized horse droppings.

Knucker.

Knucker scat.

Knucker footprints.

TRACKING TECHNIQUES.

While a practised eye is the best tool in tracking dragons, there are a number of other tools that can be useful. Chief among these, and very easy to make at home, is a tracking stick, which can help you to find even the faintest impressions made by a dragon's feet.

A TRACKING STICK.

Lay a straight stick, slightly longer than the stride of the dragon you are tracking, between a set of dragon tracks. Mark it as shown in the diagram below. In order to find the next set of footprints, lay the stick down placing the last visible set of tracks between points A and B. The next track must have fallen near the end of the stick. Rotate the stick and look for even the tiniest signs of dragon tracks.

Tie twine markers at A and B to indicate the length of the dragon footprint.

A tray of modelling clay or putty can be placed on any path used by dragons to record footprints.

C.

B.

A.

A to B: Size of footprint.
B to C: Size of stride.
A to C: Size of step interval.

a. Prepare the form.

b. Pour in plaster.

c. Remove the cast.

PLASTER CASTS.

In order to take a plaster cast of a footprint, first mix plaster-of-paris with water. Make a wooden form and press it into the ground around the print. Finally, pour in the plaster, and wait until it has dried before removing it.

A TRACKING PLATE.

Take a flat metal sheet and hold it over a candle flame until it is blackened all over with soot. Next, place the sheet where you suspect that dragons—or other creatures—may pass by. Leave the sheet for a few hours. If you are lucky, you will see dragon tracks on it when you return.

OTHER SIGNS OF DRAGON ACTIVITY.

Long, deep scratches on trees and rocks used to sharpen claws.
Bones of animals that have been torn limb from limb.
Abandoned villages burned in terrible fits of rage.

A TRACKING CAMP.

On expeditions that last several days, always remember to build your camp as far away as possible from the trails used by dragons. Remember: it is you who is supposed to be doing the tracking and sneaking up, not the dragon.

OTHER ANIMAL TRACKS.

Even though it can be particularly interesting tracking dragons, the experienced tracker is sure to come across a range of different types of footprint that have been left by other wild animals and birds. It can be useful to also be able to identify these, even if only to eliminate them as not having been made by a passing dragon.

Bear.

Crow.

Moose.

Otter.

Dog.

Elephant.

ADVANCED TRACKING EQUIPMENT.

Once upon a time the only gadget available to the master dragon tracker was a Dragon Ear Trumpet Helmet that allowed sounds to be discerned over huge distances. Today dragonologists may take advantage of a whole range of more modern scientific paraphernalia that has now become available.

All of these items of equipment may be ordered, hired or purchased from a reputable dragonological outfitter.

MALE DRAGON ATTRACTOR
[pumps out the scent of the dung of a female dragon].

DRAGON HORN
[makes a terrible roar like an angry rival dragon].

DRAGON'S DELIGHT
[makes a "baa" like a little lost lamb].

DRAGON DETECTOR
[with dragon dust, which heats up if any are about].

One useful method of approaching dragons involves the use of a dragon dummy costume, such as the one shown above. Be sure that your actions mimic those of a real dragon, or your encounter may be brought to a fiery end.

S.A.S.D. NOTE.

While the tracking techniques outlined in this book may be practised by anyone, the techniques outlined in the rest of the book are provided for information only. Make sure that you catch or train a dragon only in cases of actual need.

Remember, FATALITIES often occur as a result of young, inexperienced dragonologists being too keen to introduce themselves too soon!

HOW TO CATCH DRAGONS.

Although in the past, it was normal for western people to see almost all dragons as "problems" that needed to be "eliminated", nowadays a dragon that is a threat to humans, say by devouring them too frequently, can be easily caught in a simple dragon trap and relocated.

Provided the dragon is hungry enough no great level of sophistication is required in trap design.

APPROACHING WILD DRAGONS.

After mastering the art of following dragon tracks, it can be frustrating if, at the end of them, you find the dragon took to the skies and flew away. However, if you do find a dragon at the end, remember to approach it with care.

LOBSTER POT TRAPS.

One form of trap is called the "lobster pot." It is made of toughened steel mesh with a neck that allows inquisitive dragons in much more readily than it lets them out again.

Learning to Train Dragons.

It may come as a surprise to find that young dragons are no more difficult to train than big cats such as lions and tigers, although they can still prove highly dangerous to the uncautious. However, the training of adult dragons—which needs to be done more often—is a far harder task.

DRAGON TRAINING EQUIPMENT.

Apart from the whip—which is quite pointless as it will not hurt the dragon, but will rather enrage it—the items to the right are all part of the stock-in-trade of the modern dragon trainer.

TRAINING BABY DRAGONS.

There is a chance that a dragon chick that you have hatched yourself will take you for its parent, and copy you in the same way it would its mother. There is also a chance this will not happen, and that the chick will be merely biding its time, waiting for a chance to get you.

Iron Stool—to keep an angry dragon at bay.

Dragon Costume—to model "correct" behaviours.

Diamonds—handy little rewards.

Flameaway Hat—for saving face.

Whip—actual use can prove disastrous.

A SECURE REFUGE.

Remember it is essential to have somewhere secure to keep your dragon when it is not being trained. Some dragons can find training sessions rather trying and will be quite keen to demonstrate their anger.

Let the dragon calm down a little before resuming training.

TRAINING ADULT DRAGONS.

Adult dragons, particularly old, wise specimens that can talk, will resist all forms of training or dominance. Unless you can outwit the dragon, it is likely that a fatality— either your own or that of the dragon—is almost certain to result.

MISTREATMENT OF DRAGONS.

The sight of a dragon being tormented by a wicked trainer can be a heart-rending sight. All dragonologists must ardently seek out and expose cases of dragon mistreatment. Report all incidences of any activities such as those described below.

This circus master learned all too soon the dangers of putting his head into a hungry dragon's mouth.

A Dancing Dragon.

Tied to a stake, the poor beast is forced to "dance" for the supposed amusement of the public.

Hoop-La.

Seen at circuses, the dragon is made to fly in and out of a fiery hoop, to the applause of the crowd.

Room Guarding.

Some wicked dragonologists train captured dragons to stand guard over their homes or bedrooms.

13

A Training Regime.

Training must be regular if it is to be effective. You must be firm in your attitude. If you have decided to offer a dragon treats only when it performs some act you have trained it to do, it will be counterproductive if you then give it a treat merely because it "makes eyes" at you.

Expect repeated scorchings—especially during the early stages of a dragon's training.

STARTING OUT.

As with all animal training, it is important to remember that at first you should not bother too much about getting exact results. Indeed, at first, almost any results will do. You may find, when starting to train a dragon—say, by performing an action you hope it will copy, and offering it a treat if it does so—that merely reaching a position where the dragon does not attack you too viciously makes a very good start. You may then gradually become more demanding

REWARDS NOT PUNISHMENTS.

It is worth emphasising that a dragon must be trained by a system of offering rewards for good behaviour, rather than meting out punishments for bad behaviour. As dragons learn by example, you will find that a dragon you have treated well will treat you well in return, while one you have severely punished can become increasingly difficult.

PERFECTING YOUR TECHNIQUE.

If you manage to survive the dark days of early dragon training reasonably unscathed, then you will almost certainly have earned a good deal of respect from the dragon involved.

GOOD REASONS TO TRAIN DRAGONS.

It is acceptable to train a dragon which needs to be moved from one place to another for its own safety, or to train a youngster you are raising in order to prevent unfortunate disasters. Here are some example commands:

Fly! A dragon that is learning to fly may be taught to carry someone on its back.

Fetch! A dragon that has been relocated may be taught to "fetch" its own treasure to its new lair.

Lie Down! This command will assist in hiding the dragon should this be needed.

Roll Over! Useful for preparing the ground for your camp *en route* to the dragon's new home.

A properly trained dragon will be happy to assist you, should you require its aid.

DRAGON TRAINING CASE STUDIES:
PHINEAS FEEK'S FREAK FAIR.

These case studies show examples where dragons have had to be either rescued from wicked trainers, or trained so as to be moved. The first one concerns an American "Freak Fair" that starred not only dragons but a host of other magical creatures. Any dragonologist would have been horrified to witness the deeds Feek performed in the supposed name of "entertainment." I decided to put a stop to them at once.

Free At Last!

It was easy to wait until nightfall and then free the beasts with a group of dragonologist vigilantes, but there was one problem.

An artist's impression of Feek busy "training" one of his victims.

Thumbs Up For Drake's
DRAGON SIGNING
Lectures

"GOOD DRAGON!"
Price 1'6" for One Lesson
The DRAGON KENNELS
Pippbrook Mill, Dorking

DR. DRAKE'S
"FREEDOM"
BRACELETS & JEWELLERY

SHOW YOU CARE!
Proceeds Help Conserve & Protect Dragons.

The dragon was so used to performing for Feek that it had forgotten how to hunt. It had also forgotten how to breathe fire. A short training session resulted in the dragon being ready for release. And, after a short "reunion" with Feek, it flew happily away to begin its new life in the mountains.

DRAGON TRAINING CASE STUDIES:
OPERATION FLAME.

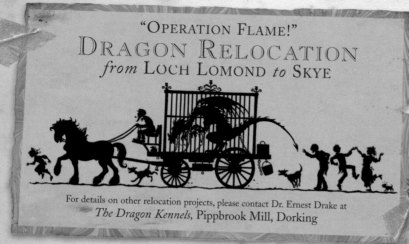

"OPERATION FLAME!"
DRAGON RELOCATION
from LOCH LOMOND *to* SKYE

For details on other relocation projects, please contact Dr. Ernest Drake at
The Dragon Kennels, Pippbrook Mill, Dorking

In Operation Flame a dragon who lived too near to human habitations had to be moved for its [and the humans'] safety. The usual method would have been to retrain the dragon but speed was of the essence.

The essence of the problem was that a dragon had taken up residence near Loch Lomond in Scotland. This loch lies near Glasgow [in terms of the distance a dragon can fly] and so it soon began to cause a problem for the local populace.

Expeditions were quickly mounted to kill the dragon. Fortunately, the Secret and Ancient Society of Dragonologists were informed, and the dragon was quickly captured and moved to the southern slopes of Ben Nevis. There, it was convinced of the benefits of moving to the more remote Cuillin Mountains on the Isle of Skye. Seeing the benefit of this, the dragon itself transported a crack team of dragonologists to the island, and soon settled down happily into its new home.

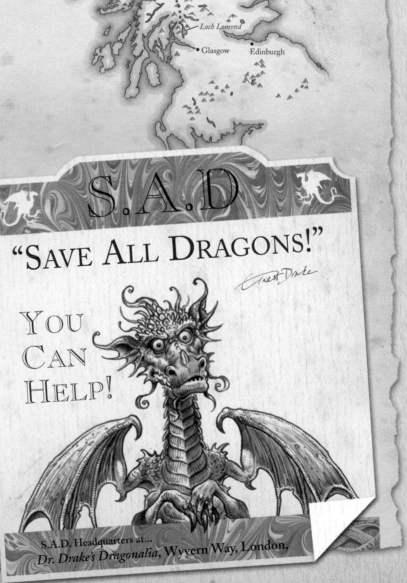

S.A.D

"SAVE ALL DRAGONS!"

Ernest Drake

YOU
CAN
HELP!

S.A.D. Headquarters at...
Dr. Drake's Dragonalia, Wyvern Way, London,

DRAGON WHISPERING & RIDDLES.

A "dragon whisperer" has a great affinity with dragons, and often uses ancient rhymes to help with training. Despite being quite hard to understand—and almost nonsensical at times—they can be highly efficacious.

CALMING

What is louder than a stone?
And faster than a snail?
Lives longer than a mayfly?
Is wider than a nail?
What flies farther than a dog?
Is blunter than a sword?
Is fiercer than water?
And has a treasure hoard?

Answer: a dragon

ROUSING

Dragons rise and dragons roar,
Dragons, dragons at the door.
Dragons flap and dragons fly,
Dragons, dragons passing by.
Dragons come and dragons go,
Dragons, dragons don't say no.
Dragons here and dragons there,
Dragons, dragons everywhere.

BEFRIENDING

Draco-raco draco-rac,
Treasure's leisure's pleasure,
Draco-raco draco-drac,
Pleasure's treasure's leisure,
Draco-raco raco-drac,
Leisure's pleasure's treasure,
Aco-draco aco-drac,
Treasure's pleasure's leisure!

WARNING

I told you once, I told you twice
I told you once again
You said you could, you said you would
Not do the thing again.
I tell you no, I tell you, go!
Don't let it be in vain!

PUTTING TO SLEEP

Go to sleep my wyvern,
Close your weary eyes,
Fall asleep so deeply deep
Give in to sleepy sighs.

Go to sleep my wyvern,
Rest your weary head,
Lay it down with not a frown
Upon your treasure bed.

SUMMONING

Come forth scaly beast,
Come forth and feast.
Come forth and roar,
Come to my door.
Come forth and fly,
Come forth and cry.
Come forth and play,
But come forth today!

As every experienced dragonologist knows, dragons who can talk simply cannot resist a riddle challenge. However, as every inexperienced dragonologist soon finds out, they are usually very familiar with the old riddles and are liable to use them to their own advantage. The solution? In order to become a Master Riddler, you must begin by unravelling some of the classic riddles. See how you get on!

Oft I must strive with wind and wave,
battle them both when under the sea.
I feel out the bottom, a foreign land.
In lying still I am strong in the strife;
If I fail in that they are stronger than I,
And wrenching me loose, soon put me to rout.
They wish to capture what I must keep.
I can master them both if my grip holds out,
If the rocks bring succour and lend support,
Strength in the struggle.
Ask me my name!

The part of the bird
that is not in the sky,
which can swim in the ocean
and always stay dry.
What is it?

The wave, over the wave, a weird
thing I saw,
Through-wrought, and wonderful
ornate:
A wonder on the waves, water
become bone.

What gets wetter the more it dries?

What does man love more than life,
Fear more than death or mortal strife,
What the poor have, the rich require,
And what contented men desire,
What misers spend, and spendthrifts save,
And all men carry to the grave?

Weight in my belly,
Trees on my back,
Nails in my ribs,
Feet I do lack.

What am I?

Appendix II.
A Tracking Journal.

T he experienced dragon tracker is always careful to keep notes of his tracking experiences. Below you can see a sample page from such a journal—on the next page there is a blank version that you may copy to use yourself.

DRAGON:	Wyvern
DATE:	15th September 1875
PLACE:	Box Hill, Dorking
AGE:	10 years
SIZE:	20ft

NOTE: The experienced tracker will practise drawing dragons in the field whenever the opportunity arises. Quick pencil studies of head, wing, tail and leg formations can be invaluable aids to species identification when you get home.

Here are some close-ups of various items of a dragon's "equipment".

Claw.

Eye.

Wingtip.

Horn.

Detail of scales.

FIRST SIGHTING:	On the steep escarpment to the south of the main hill.
ACTIVITY:	Digging up flints.
TRACK MARKS:	Footprint found in clay near the base of the main hill.
OTHER SIGNS OF DRAGON ACTIVITY:	Many trees have been burned or torn up. Usual signs of scat. An egg.

OTHER NOTES:

What a remarkable tracking experience! I was only expecting to find a knucker, but a young wyvern has arrived at Box Hill in Surrey and seems fascinated with digging up flints. He has brought an egg with him [his brother or sister?] He has torn up half a hillside so far. How did it arrive from Africa? I must find out more!

MY TRACKING JOURNAL.

Start your journal by making a sketch of a dragon you have tracked. Then, complete it by filling in the relevant details so that you have a complete record.

DRAGON:

DATE:

PLACE:

AGE:

SIZE:

From *Tracking and Taming Dragons* by Dr. Ernest Drake.

FIRST SIGHTING:

ACTIVITY:

TRACK MARKS:

OTHER SIGNS OF
DRAGON ACTIVITY:

OTHER NOTES:

AFTERWORD.

Remember that, while tracking dragons is an enjoyable pursuit that can teach you a great deal about these noble creatures, taming them is another matter. As ever, I feel compelled to remind all students of dragonology that their main goal must remain the conservation and protection, not only of dragons, but of all the magnificent creatures of the earth.

Yours in Dragonology,

Ernest Drake